Goldie
the Sunshine
Fairy

by Daisy Meadows

illustrated by Georgie Ripper

Join the Rainbow Magic Reading Challenge!

Read the story and collect your fairy points to climb the Reading Rainbow online. Turn to the back of the book for details!

This book is worth 5 points.

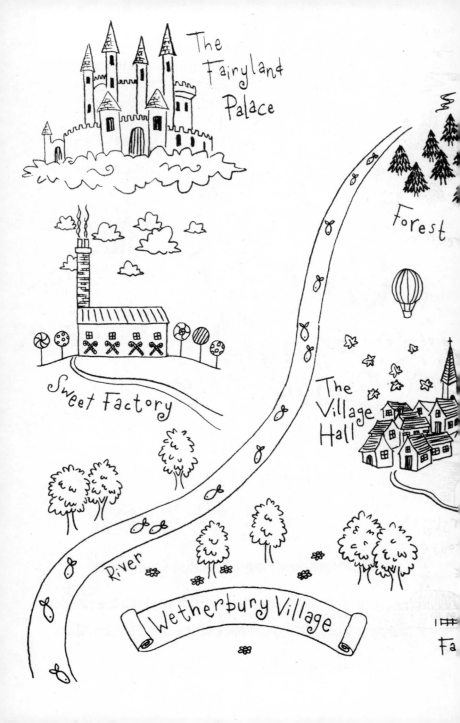

RAINBOW
magic ®
The Weather Fairies

Dedicated to Liss Brothwell,
who is a little ray of sunshine

Special thanks to
Sue Mongredien

ORCHARD BOOKS

First published in Great Britain in 2004 by Orchard Books
This edition published in 2016 by The Watts Publishing Group

3 5 7 9 10 8 6 4 2

© 2016 Rainbow Magic Limited.
© 2016 HIT Entertainment Limited.
Illustrations © Georgie Ripper 2004

HiT entertainment

The moral rights of the author and illustrator have been asserted.
All characters and events in this publication, other than those clearly in the public domain,
are fictitious and any resemblance to real persons, living or dead, is purely coincidental.

A CIP catalogue record for this book is available from the British Library.

ISBN 978 1 40834 861 1

Printed in Great Britain by CPI Group (UK) Ltd, Croydon CR0 4YY

MIX
Paper from
responsible sources
FSC
www.fsc.org   FSC® C104740

The paper and board used in this book are made from wood from responsible sources

Orchard Books
An imprint of Hachette Children's Group
Part of The Watts Publishing Group Limited
Carmelite House, 50 Victoria Embankment, London EC4Y 0DZ

An Hachette UK Company
www.hachette.co.uk
www.hachettechildrens.co.uk

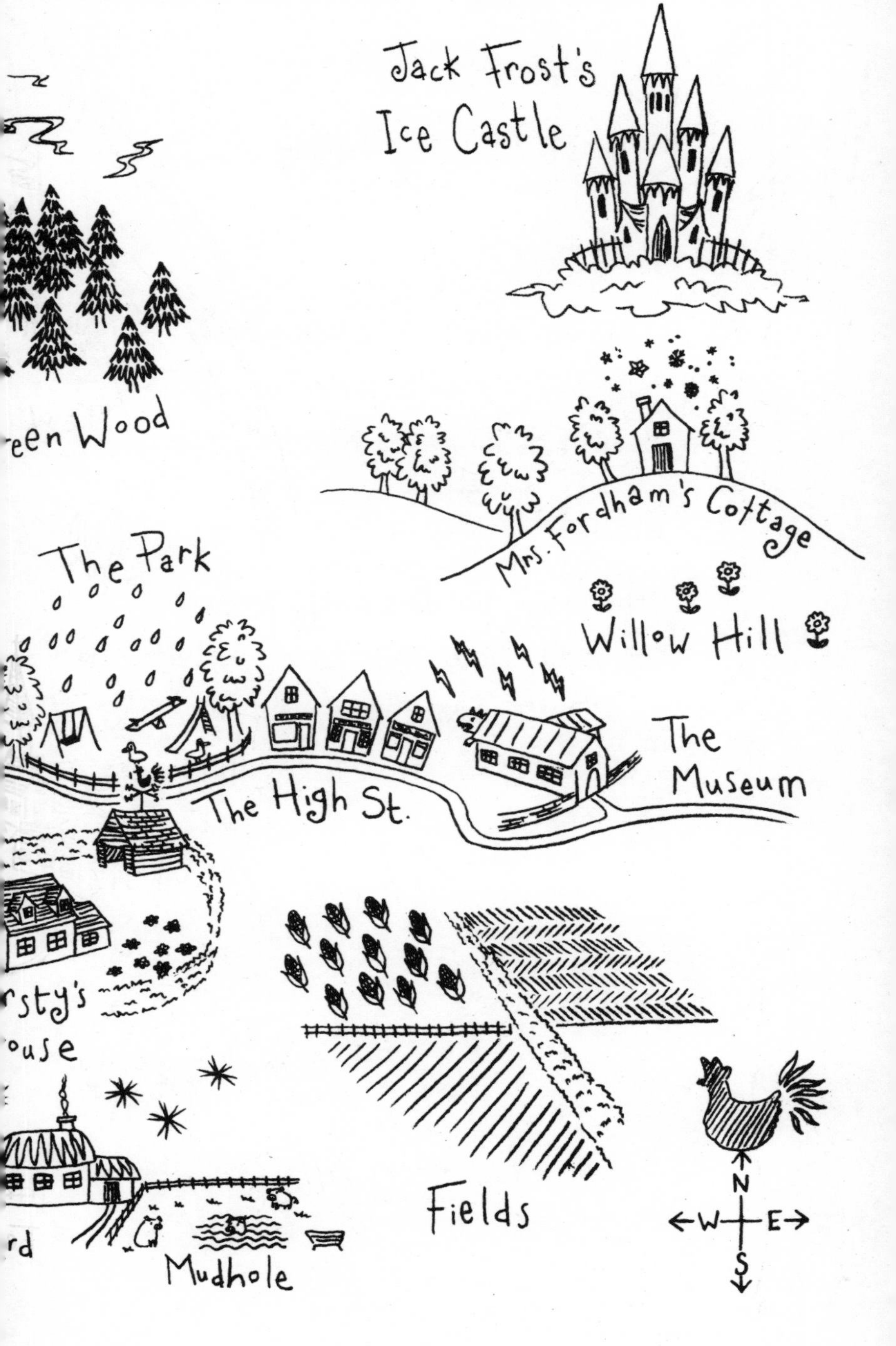

Jack Frost's
Ice Castle

een Wood

Mrs. Fordham's Cottage

The Park

Willow Hill

The
Museum

The High St.

rsty's
ouse

Fields

rd

Mudhole

N
←W ✛ E→
S

Goblins green and goblins small,
I cast this spell to make you tall.
As high as the palace you shall grow.
My icy magic makes it so.

Then steal Doodle's magic feathers,
Used by the fairies to make all weathers.
Climate chaos I have planned
On Earth, and here, in Fairyland!

Contents

A Sunny Spell

"I feel as if I'm about to melt," said Rachel Walker happily.

It was a hot summer afternoon and she and her friend, Kirsty Tate, were enjoying the sunshine in Kirsty's back garden. A bumblebee buzzed lazily around Mrs Tate's sunflowers, and a single breath of wind whispered through the yellow rose bushes.

The weather had been so warm and sunny, Mr and Mrs Tate had given the girls permission to camp out in the garden that night. Kirsty looked up from a jumble of tent poles and bright orange material she was sorting through. "It's been a perfect day," she agreed. "Let's hope tonight is perfect, too. I don't fancy lying out here in the rain, do you?"

Rachel laughed, and started untangling tent pegs with her friend. "I think I'd rather have a shower in the morning, not in the middle of the night," she agreed.

Kirsty held up some poles. "Right.
How do we put this thing together,
then?" she asked brightly.

Rachel scratched her head. "Well..."
she began.

"Need some help?" came a voice
from behind them.

"Dad!" said Kirsty in relief. "Yes,
please. We—" She burst out laughing
as she looked at her father.

Rachel turned to see
what was so funny. She
had to bite her lip not to
laugh, too. For there,
standing in front of
them, was Mr Tate,
wearing the most
enormous sunglasses
she had ever seen.

Mr Tate was looking very pleased. He waggled the glasses up and down on his nose. "Do you like my new shades?" he asked.

"Well, yes," Kirsty said, trying to keep a straight face. "They're very... summery."

Mr Tate knelt down and started putting the tent together. "The weather has been strange all week, I didn't know whether to buy them or not," he said. "I hope it doesn't start snowing again!"

Rachel and Kirsty looked at each other but didn't say anything. They shared a very special secret. They knew *exactly* why the weather had been so strange – Jack Frost had been messing it all up.

Doodle, the fairy weather-vane cockerel, usually looked after the weather with his seven magic tail feathers. But Jack Frost had cast a spell to make his goblin servants bigger and sent them to steal Doodle's feathers. Without them, the weather had gone completely haywire. Rachel and Kirsty were helping the Weather Fairies to get them back, but until that time, Doodle was just an ordinary iron weather-vane on top of the Tates' barn.

Yesterday, with the help of Pearl
the Cloud Fairy, Kirsty and Rachel
had returned the Cloud Feather to
Doodle. But there were still four
feathers left to find.

"There!" said Mr Tate, stepping back
and admiring the finished tent. "It's all
yours."

"Thanks, Dad," Kirsty said as he
walked away. She put two sleeping
bags inside the tent and then flopped
down on the grass. "Phew!"
she whistled. "It's still
so hot! I hope it cools
down soon, or we'll
never be able to
sleep in there."
Rachel was frowning
and looking at her watch.

"Kirsty," she said slowly. "Have you noticed where the sun is?"

Kirsty looked up and pointed. "Right there, in the sky," she replied helpfully.

"Yes, but look how high it is," Rachel insisted. "It hasn't even *started* setting yet."

Kirsty glanced at her watch. "But it's half-past seven," she said. Now she was frowning, too. "So that can't be right."

Rachel had just opened her mouth to
reply, when suddenly there was a loud
Pop! "What was that?" she whispered.

Pop! Pop! Pop!

"It sounds like it's coming from the
other side of the hedge," Kirsty
answered, her eyes wide. "But there's
only a cornfield over there."

Pop! Pop! Pop!

Curiously, the girls peeped over the hedge to see what was making all the noise. And then they both gasped out loud.

Goldie Drops In

"I don't believe it," Kirsty said, rubbing her eyes. "Is that what I think it is?"

Pop! Pop! Pop!

Rachel nodded. "Popcorn," she breathed.

It was an amazing sight. The sun was so hot that the corn in the field was literally cooking – and turning into popcorn!

19

Both girls stared as golden puffs of corn
bounced everywhere. It was just
as if the field was one
enormous saucepan.
A delicious smell of
popcorn drifted over
the hedge, and both
girls sniffed hungrily.

Kirsty and Rachel looked
at each other, and grinned.

"There's definitely magic
in the air," Kirsty said.

"It must be the goblin
with the Sunshine Feather,"
Rachel agreed, feeling her
heart beat faster with excitement.

Both girls peered hard at the
field, hoping to spot a goblin lurking
somewhere, but it was difficult to see

clearly through the blizzard of popcorn.
It was still tumbling and twirling
in the sky, like a sandstorm.
Rachel suddenly grabbed
Kirsty's hand.
"Look!" she cried.
Kirsty stared.
Darting above the
corn was a twinkling
yellow light. It was
zigzagging through the air
between the flying pieces of
popcorn and heading straight
towards them. As it came
closer, the air above the field
seemed to glitter with a thousand
tiny sparkles. Both girls could see a
pair of delicate golden wings beating
quickly, and the glimmer of a tiny wand.

"It's Goldie the Sunshine Fairy,"
whispered Rachel in delight.

They held their breath as the fairy
weaved in and out of the bouncing
corn, neatly dodging each piece. Then
she swooped down to land on the
hedge in front of them. "Phew!" she
laughed. "Talk about a bumpy ride!"

Kirsty and Rachel
watched as Goldie
shook popcorn dust
from her glittering,
golden-edged
wings. Her face
was framed by
long, curly, blonde
hair, and she wore a
gauzy dress in fiery reds,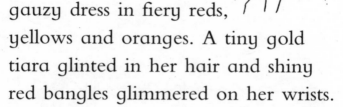
yellows and oranges. A tiny gold
tiara glinted in her hair and shiny
red bangles glimmered on her wrists.

"Hello again," said Goldie. "I've
been hearing all about how you've
helped Crystal, Abigail and Pearl.
You've done brilliantly!"

Rachel and Kirsty grinned at
each other proudly.

"The goblin who has the Sunshine Feather can't be far away," Goldie went on, looking up at the sky where the sun was still blazing as brightly as ever.

"That's what we thought," Kirsty said. "There's a farm on the other side of this field. Shall we start looking there?"

"Good idea," Goldie replied cheerfully. But then her face fell as she looked at the cornfield again. Popcorn was still whizzing around like hot white missiles. "Is there another way across the field, though?"

Goblin on the Loose!

Goldie sighed. "I don't fancy dodging that popcorn again," she said. She leaned back to examine a scorch mark on one of her wings. "I almost burned myself last time."

"There's a lane that runs down the side of the field to the farm," Kirsty told her. "We'll ask Mum if we can go for a quick walk before bedtime."

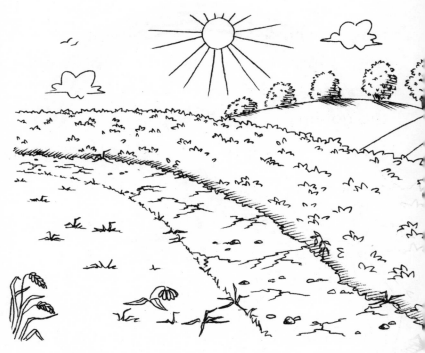

Minutes later, the three of them were on
their way. The air was practically
shimmering with heat. There were cracks
in the ground where the earth had
become hardened by the sun,
flowers wilted in the hedgerow, and the
grass was turning dry and brown. There

wasn't even the slightest gasp of wind now. Once they reached the farm, the girls and Goldie started searching for the goblin.

First they peeped into the stables.
Two very hot-looking horses were
sheltering from the sun. "Hello," Goldie
said. "I don't suppose you've seen a
goblin hanging around, have you?"

One of the horses shook her mane.

"All we've seen is this stable," she said.
"And there are no goblins in here."

"It's too hot to go out," the other
horse whinnied.

Next the girls and Goldie slipped into the cowshed. The cows were all half-asleep in the heat, and quite grumpy at being disturbed. There was no goblin.

At last the three friends came to the duck pond. They wondered if the goblin might be cooling off in the water, but there was no sign of him – or the Sunshine Feather.

"You should ask the pigs," a duck quacked helpfully from a shady spot in the reeds.

"They've been grumbling all day about something or other. And pigs are nosy. If there's a goblin on the farm, they'll know about it."

Goldie thanked the duck politely.

"I think I can hear the pigs over here," Rachel said, leading the way around the side of the farmhouse.

Soon they could all hear the grunting. The duck was right, the pigs seemed very upset about something. They all turned to look curiously at Goldie, though, when she flew over to speak to them.

Goldie fluttered down to perch on the biggest pig's snout. "What's the problem?" she asked kindly.

The pig squinted at the golden fairy in front of his little blue eyes. "It's like this," he began, in a cross, squeaky kind of voice. "It's been so hot that the farmer topped up the mudhole with water, so that us pigs could keep nice and cool." He twitched his ears indignantly. "But someone else has pinched our spot in the mud – and he won't let us in!"

"It's not fair," a piglet squealed, running up to Rachel and Kirsty. "It's not fa-a-a-air!"

"It certainly isn't," Kirsty agreed, giving him a pat.

"It sounds like just the kind of trick a goblin would play!" Rachel pointed out. "Where is the mudhole?"

The pigs gave directions and the girls set off with Goldie flying above their heads. Rachel crossed her fingers. She felt quite sure that they would find a goblin in the mud. Who else would be mean enough to

stop the pigs from wallowing in their own mud pool?

They hadn't been walking for very long when they heard someone singing in a croaky, tuneless voice:

"I've been having so much fun
Blasting out this golden sun.
It's roasting, toasting, popcorn weather.
Oh, how I love my Sunshine Feather!"

Kirsty, Rachel and Goldie dived behind a nearby tree at once, and carefully peeped out. There, right in the middle of the mudhole, covered in thick, wet mud, was an extremely cheerful goblin. He waved the Sunshine Feather in the air as he sang, and each time it moved, golden sunbeams flooded from its tip, making the air feel even hotter.

When he got to the end of his song, he started all over again, splashing his feet in the mud in time to the words. "I've been having so much fun..."

"What shall we do?" Kirsty whispered. The goblin was holding the feather so tightly, it looked like it would be impossible to take it from him.

Goldie twirled around in frustration.

"I hate seeing him with my Sunshine Feather," she muttered, folding her arms across her chest. "Look, he's got it all muddy!"

Rachel frowned. "Maybe we could distract him somehow, then dash over and grab the feather while he's looking the other way."

"I don't fancy dashing through all that slippery mud," Kirsty said quietly, eyeing it doubtfully. "We'll probably fall over. And look, he's right in the middle of it. He'll be able to spot us coming way before we get there."

They drew further away from the mudhole so that they could discuss their next move without fear of the goblin

overhearing. After a few minutes,
Rachel held up a hand. "Ssshh! What's
that noise?" she hissed in alarm.

A Bamboozled Goblin

Kirsty, Rachel and Goldie held their breath as they listened to the strange new sound. It was a loud, wheezing, rumbling kind of noise, somewhere between a grunt and a hiss. Grumble-sshhh, it went. Grumble-sshhh. Grumble-sshhh...

It was coming from the direction of

the mudhole. Kirsty and Rachel crept
back to the tree and peeped out from
behind it, wondering what sort of
terrifying creature they were going
to see.

When Rachel saw what was making
the noise, though, she had to clap her
hand over her mouth to stop herself
laughing out loud. The wheezy
rumble was nothing more than the
goblin – snoring!

"At least he isn't singing any more,"
Kirsty laughed.

Goldie fluttered her
wings hopefully when
she saw that the
goblin was asleep,
and she flew a little
closer to the Sunshine
Feather. But her face
fell when she saw just
how tightly the goblin
was clutching the feather to

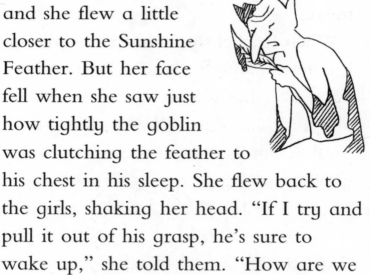

his chest in his sleep. She flew back to
the girls, shaking her head. "If I try and
pull it out of his grasp, he's sure to
wake up," she told them. "How are we
going to get that feather?"

A smile appeared on Kirsty's face.
"Maybe we could..." she began
thoughtfully. Then she grinned broadly.
"Yes! That could work!" she declared.

Without another word, she began running back towards her house. "Back in a minute," she called over her shoulder.

Rachel and Goldie watched her go. They were both dying to know what Kirsty was up to. Luckily, they didn't have to wait long for her return. And when she came back, she looked quite different!

"What *is* she wearing?" Goldie murmured to Rachel as they saw Kirsty running towards them.

"Her dad's sunglasses," Rachel replied, staring at her friend with great interest. She was starting to wonder if Kirsty had been in the sun for too long. Why had she brought the enormous sunglasses with her? And why was she carrying a fishing rod?

Kirsty grinned at the confused expressions on their faces. "I'll explain everything," she promised, reaching up to rest the fishing rod in the tree. "First, we need to shrink to fairy size, Rachel." Both Kirsty and Rachel had been given beautiful gold lockets by the Fairy Queen. Inside each locket was magical fairy dust. A tiny pinch of the sparkling dust was enough to turn the girls into fairies in the twinkling of an eye!

Kirsty and Rachel
sprinkled themselves
with fairy dust. It
glittered a bright
sunshine-yellow in
the light and then
– whoosh – they
were getting smaller
and smaller
and smaller. The tree
next to them became
enormous as the
girls shrank to the
size of Goldie.

Kirsty and
Rachel fluttered
their wings in
delight. They both
loved being fairies.

"Now then," Kirsty said. "Fly up to the tree and I'll tell you my plan."

They all perched by the fishing rod, and Goldie and Rachel watched as Kirsty's nimble fingers balanced the sunglasses on the end of the fishing hook.

"We're going to let the fishing line out slowly," Kirsty told them quietly, "and lower the sunglasses onto the goblin's nose."

"Why?" Rachel wanted to know.

"Do you think they'll suit him?" Goldie asked.

Kirsty shook her head, trying not to laugh. "With sunglasses on, everything will look dark to him," she whispered. "With a bit of luck, he'll think the Sunshine Feather has broken!"

Goldie clapped her hands in delight.

"Oh, what a good idea!" she cried. "I do love to play tricks on those mean old goblins."

Very carefully, Kirsty, Rachel and Goldie turned the wheel of the fishing rod and lowered the sunglasses all the way down to the goblin. Kirsty held her breath as the sunglasses landed right on the end of his nose. Perfect! They reeled in the fishing line and then Goldie waved her wand to release a stream of magical, sunny fairy dust. Little golden sparkles fizzed and popped like firecrackers around the goblin's head until he woke with a start.

He opened his eyes and blinked when he saw that everything seemed to have gone dark. "My feather's broken!" he moaned, giving it a shake. "Shine, you stupid sun!" he commanded.

Of course, the Sunshine Feather wasn't broken at all. As soon as the goblin shook it, the sun shone more brilliantly than ever. But as far as the goblin could see, the world remained in darkness.

He waved the feather again. "I said, 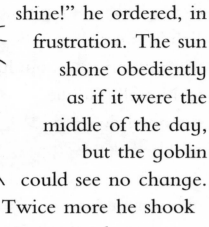 shine!" he ordered, in frustration. The sun shone obediently as if it were the middle of the day, but the goblin could see no change. Twice more he shook the feather and twice more the sun shone hotter and brighter, but through the sunglasses, the goblin saw only twilight. As far as he knew, the Sunshine Feather was having no effect. "Broken!" the goblin finally announced crossly, and he threw the feather away in disgust.

Goldie shot out of the tree at once, like a little golden firework. While the goblin was still muttering gloomily to himself, Goldie swooped down and grabbed the feather. "Thank you!" she sang happily, hugging it tightly as she flew back to the girls. Kirsty's plan had worked!

With another sprinkle of fairy dust, Rachel and Kirsty turned themselves human again and started scrambling down from the tree with the fishing rod.

The goblin spotted them and jumped to his feet. As he did so, the sunglasses bounced on his nose. "Sunglasses?" he exclaimed, sounding puzzled as he reached up to grab the glasses. He pushed them onto the top of his head and peered at the girls, blinking in the dazzling sunlight. "You tricked me!" he yelled in fury when he saw Goldie clutching the Sunshine Feather. "Come back with that feather!"

Kirsty and Rachel looked at each other fearfully. Now that Jack Frost's goblins were so big, they seemed more scary than ever. And this one looked very angry at having been outwitted.

He shook his fist and ran straight towards the girls.

"*Run!*" shouted Kirsty.

Happy Pigs

Rachel grabbed Kirsty's hand
and they both ran towards the
farmhouse as fast as they could.
The goblin was right behind them,
making a horrible growling sound
in his throat.

"Give me back that feather! Give
it back!" he screamed angrily.

Rachel's heart thumped painfully in her chest as she ran. The goblin was closing on them. She could hear his breathing, hoarse and ragged. The goblin stretched out his hand to grab her and she gasped as she felt his fingertips brush her shoulder.

"Got y—" he began. Then his voice turned from anger to confusion. "Hey! What's happening?"

With a swirl of dancing sunbeams,
Goldie had waved the Sunshine Feather
and pointed it straight at the goblin. At
once, the sun beat down fiercely upon
him – and the thick mud that
smothered him started drying rapidly.
As his legs became stiff and heavy with
the solidifying mud, the goblin slowed.
Then, as the mud set hard, the goblin
found he couldn't move at all.

"No-o-o-!" he wailed in despair.

Despite having been so scared just a few seconds earlier, the girls found themselves smiling at the sight of the goblin. "He's a goblin statue!" Rachel exclaimed, laughing.

Only his eyes moved now. They flicked back and forth wildly as the goblin glared first at the girls, and then at Goldie who was fluttering beside them. Kirsty noticed her dad's sunglasses on top of the goblin's head. She took a cautious step towards him. And another. The goblin remained motionless, so she marched right up to him and carefully took the glasses.

"I'll have these back now, I think," she said. "If I'd known how useful these sunglasses would be, I'd never have laughed at Dad for wearing them!" she told Rachel.

Goldie and the girls made their way back to the farmhouse where the pigs were waiting expectantly.

"The mudhole is all yours again," Goldie said to the pigs in her sweet silvery voice. "You'll find a new goblin scarecrow nearby," she added. "But don't worry. He won't be in any hurry to go back into the mud."

The pigs grunted joyfully and started trotting off in search of their cool mud pool. The smallest piglet nuzzled around Kirsty and Rachel's legs before he went. "Thank you," he squealed happily.

Rachel watched them go. "What will happen to the goblin?" she asked. "He won't have to stay there for ever, will he?"

Goldie's eyes twinkled mischievously. "Not for ever, no," she said. "He'll get out of the mud as soon as it rains." She smiled cheerfully. "Jack Frost won't be pleased with him when he finds out we've got the Sunshine Feather back, though!"

Twilight Magic

Now that they were out of danger,
Goldie waved the Sunshine Feather
with an expert flourish and the sun
began to set – just as it was supposed
to. The girls watched as the sky was
flooded with orange and pink and a
rich deep red.

"Let's take the Sunshine Feather back

to Doodle," Kirsty said happily. "And then we'd better go to bed!"

Rachel was yawning. "It's been another busy day, hasn't it?" she smiled.

With the sun setting, the warmth was quickly ebbing away and the girls soon found themselves shivering in their thin T-shirts. Goldie fluttered above them with the Sunshine Feather, tapping it gently to sprinkle a few sunbeams onto their bare arms to keep them warm.

It was almost dark by the time they got back to Kirsty's garden. They could just about see the silhouette of Doodle perched on the barn roof.

Goldie flew up to give the cockerel back his magic feather. As she did so, Doodle came to life, his fiery feathers glowing brilliant colours in the twilight. He turned to look at Rachel and Kirsty. "Will come—" he squawked urgently. But, before he could say any more, the magic drained away, his colours faded and he became a rusty old weather-vane once again.

Each time the girls managed to
return one of Doodle's feathers, the
cockerel came to life for a few brief
moments and squawked a couple
of words. Rachel frowned as she
pieced together all the words that
Doodle had said to them so far.
"Beware! Jack Frost will come..."
she murmured, feeling an icy shiver
down her spine as if Jack Frost
was already there. "It's a warning,
Kirsty. Let's hope he's not coming
soon!"

Goldie looked worried. "Take care,
girls. And thank you for everything,"
she said. She blew them a stream
of fairy kisses that sparkled in the
darkening sky. "I must go back
to Fairyland now. Goodbye!"

Kirsty and Rachel watched Goldie fly away until she was nothing more than a tiny golden speck in the distance. Then, just as they were about to get ready for bed, they heard footsteps and Mr Tate came out of the house. He was looking around, a puzzled expression on his face. "Did I just hear a cockerel crowing?" he asked.

"A cockerel? At this time of day?" Kirsty replied innocently.

Mr Tate frowned. "I must be hearing things," he said, turning to go back inside. "Good night, girls. Sleep well." Then he glanced up at Doodle as he headed back towards the house. "I'm sure that weather-vane had a smaller tail," he muttered, then shook his head. "Seeing things as well! Definitely time to call it a night..."

Kirsty and Rachel smiled at each other. "Only three more feathers to find," Kirsty said. "I wonder which one will be next!"

**Now it's time for Kirsty and
Rachel to help...**

Evie the Mist Fairy

Read on for a sneak peek...

"Wake up, sleepy head!" cried Kirsty Tate
to her friend, Rachel, as she jumped out of
bed and started to dress.

Rachel Walker was asleep in the spare
bed in Kirsty's room. She was staying with
Kirsty and her parents in the village of
Wetherbury. Sleepily, she rolled over and
opened her eyes. "I was dreaming that we
were back in Fairyland," she told Kirsty.
"The weather was topsy-turvy – sunny
and snowing all at the same time – and
Doodle was trying to sort it out." Doodle,
the fairies' magic weather cockerel, had

been on Rachel's mind a lot lately, because she and Kirsty were on an important fairy mission!

Each day in Fairyland, with the help of the Weather Fairies, Doodle used his magic tail feathers to organise the weather. Each of the seven magic feathers controlled a different kind of weather, and each of the seven Weather Fairies was responsible for working with one feather in particular. The system worked perfectly until mean old Jack Frost sent seven goblins to steal Doodle's magic feathers.

The goblins ran off into the human world with one feather each, and when poor Doodle followed them out of Fairyland, he found himself transformed into a rusty metal weather-vane. The Queen of the Fairies had asked Rachel and Kirsty to help find the magic feathers and return them to Doodle.

Meanwhile, Fairyland's weather was all mixed up – and the goblins had been using the feathers to cause weather chaos in the human world too.

"Poor Doodle," Kirsty said, looking out of the window at the old barn where the cockerel was perched. Her dad had found Doodle lying in the park, and thinking he was an ordinary weather vane, Mr Tate had brought him home and put him on the barn roof.

"Hopefully we'll find another magic feather today," Kirsty continued. "We've already found four of the stolen feathers. We just need to find the other three and then Doodle will get his magic back."

"Yes," Rachel agreed, brightening at the

thought. "But I have to go home in three days, so we don't have long!" As she gazed out at the blue sky, a wisp of silvery mist caught her eye. "Look, that cloud is shaped just like a feather!" she said.

Kirsty looked where Rachel was pointing. "I can't see anything."

Rachel looked again. The wispy shape had vanished. "Perhaps I imagined it," she sighed, turning away to dress.

The memory of the dream fizzed in her tummy like lemonade bubbles. It felt like a magical start to the day.

She loved staying with Kirsty and sharing fairy adventures with her. The girls had met whilst on holiday on Rainspell Island with their parents.

That was when they had first helped the fairies. On that occasion, Jack Frost had cast a nasty spell to banish the Rainbow Fairies from Fairyland, and the girls had helped all seven of them get safely home...

Read Evie the Mist Fairy to find out what adventures are in store for Kirsty and Rachel!

Meet the
Friendship Fairies

When Jack Frost steals the Friendship Fairies' magical objects, BFFs everywhere are in trouble! Can Rachel and Kirsty help save the magic of friendship?

www.rainbowmagicbooks.co.uk

RAINBOW magic

Calling all parents, carers and teachers!
The Rainbow Magic fairies are here to help
your child enter the magical world of reading.
Whatever reading stage they are at, there's
a Rainbow Magic book for everyone!
Here is Lydia the Reading Fairy's guide to
supporting your child's journey at all levels.

Starting Out
1 Our Rainbow Magic Beginner Readers are perfect for first-time readers who are just beginning to develop reading skills and confidence. Approved by teachers, they contain a full range of educational levelling, as well as lively full-colour illustrations.

Developing Readers
2 Rainbow Magic Early Readers contain longer stories and wider vocabulary for building stamina and growing confidence. These are adaptations of our most popular Rainbow Magic stories, specially developed for younger readers in conjunction with an Early Years reading consultant, with full-colour illustrations.

Going Solo
3 The Rainbow Magic chapter books – a mixture of series and one-off specials – contain accessible writing to encourage your child to venture into reading independently. These highly collectible and much-loved magical stories inspire a love of reading to last a lifetime.

www.rainbowmagicbooks.co.uk

"Rainbow Magic got my daughter reading chapter books. Great sparkly covers, cute fairies and traditional stories full of magic that she found impossible to put down" – Mother of Edie (6 years)

"Florence LOVES the Rainbow Magic books. She really enjoys reading now"
Mother of Florence (6 years)

Read along the Reading Rainbow!

Well done – you have completed the book!

This book was worth 1 star.

See how far you have climbed on the Reading Rainbow.
The more books you read, the more stars you can colour in
and the closer you will be to becoming a Royal Fairy!

Do you want to print your own Reading Rainbow?

1) Go to the Rainbow Magic website

2) Download and print out the poster

3) Colour in a star for every book you finish
and climb the Reading Rainbow

4) For every step up the rainbow,
you can download your very own certificate

There's all this and lots more at
rainbowmagicbooks.co.uk

You'll find activities, stories, a special newsletter
AND you can search for the fairy with your name!